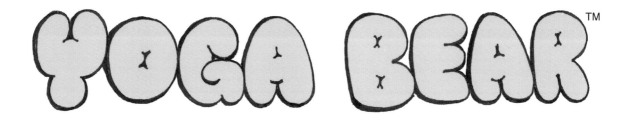

Yoga Bear™ Teddy Bear Yoga: Breathe In, Breathe Out
Summary: Yoga poses easily illustrated for children and adults

ID: 978-1-300-71666-2

Special thanks to Hisako Naito for inspiration,
and Kara Mattheisen for layout and production assistance.

My name is YOGA BEAR™. I've been doing yoga since I was a little cub. I like to stay healthy by breathing, stretching and wiggling.

Copy my poses, which are called asanas in the Sanskrit language. When you hold the asanas, remember to keep breathing. Never hold a pose if it hurts.

Smile. Breathe. Feel your body move. Remember to keep breathing!

Remember to try this pose with both your right and left leg on top!

BREATHE OUT

LOTUS POSE

पद्मासन

Padmāsana

COW POSE

व्यघ्रसन

Bidalāsana

CAT POSE

जर्यंअसन

Marjaryāsana

MOUNTAIN POSE

ताडासन

Tādāsana

Remember to
try this pose on
both sides!

BREATHE
OUT

SIDE STRETCH

अर्धचन्द्रासन

Parighāsana

UPWARD STRETCH

समस्थिति

Urdhva Hastāsana

FORWARD BEND

उत्तानासन

Uttānāsana

BREATHE IN

TABLE TOP

अर्घउत्तानासन

Ardha Uttanāsana

PLANK POSE

चतुरङ्गदण्डासन

Caturaṅga Daṇḍāsana

COBRA POSE

भुजङ्गासन

Bhujaṅgāsana

DOWNWARD DOG

अधोमुखश्वानासन

Adho Mukha Śvānāsana

CHAIR POSE

उत्कटासन

Utkaṭāsana

Remember to try
this pose on
both sides!

BREATHE
OUT

TRIANGLE POSE

त्रिकोणासन

Trikoṇāsana

Remember to try
this pose on
both sides!

WARRIOR 1

वीरभद्रासन

Vīrabhadrāsana I

WARRIOR 2

वीरभद्रासन ॥

Vīrabhadrāsana II

WHEEL POSE

चक्रासन

Chakrāsana

PLOW POSE

हलासन

Halāsana

BUTTERFLY POSE

बद्धकोणासन

Baddha Koṇāsana

SEATED STRADDLE

कूर्मासन

Upavistha Koṇāsana

HERO POSE

वीरासन

Vīrāsana

CHILD'S POSE

बालासन

Bālāsana

BREATHE IN

HAPPY BABY

बालासन

Ananda Balāsana

CORPSE POSE

शवासन

Śavāsana

SALUTATION SEAL

अञ्जलिमुद्रा

Namaste

A Salutation is a greeting. When we say hello or goodbye we press our hands together over our hearts with loving kindness.

Namaste means "My spirit bows to your spirit."
We can use it to say good-bye. "Namaste!"

GLOSSARY

The word YOGA means "to unify" or "to yoke." The practice of YOGA unites breath with body movement and focus in our minds.

ASANA is the Sanskrit word for a YOGA pose. The Sanskrit name for each pose is included in this book and ends with the word ASANA. When possible, the written Sanskrit word is also included.

YOGA BEAR™ teaches us to relax and have fun while we wiggle and move our body by practicing yoga. Look carefully at the drawings. Where are YOGA BEAR's™ paws? Are they facing up or down? Where is YOGA BEAR's™ tail? Is it tucked in or sticking out? These are clues for you to use when you copy the poses.

Never hold a pose if it hurts. Always keep breathing. Take a YOGA class to learn more about each of these ASANAS and more!